1.

Ben had always loved to watch the winged creatures that dotted the sky. In his youth, he would sit for hours on a clear summer day, watching the birds fly around on the myriad journeys across the sky. He saw the large eagles make their way to points unknown, imagining himself flying with them.

What it must be like to feel the cool air blowing across your face, looking down upon the ant-like creatures known as humans. He often found himself standing on the end of the old wooden bridge that crossed the river near his home, his arms outstretched, wondering what would happen if he jumped and found that he could fly like his friends in the sky.

He never did take that sudden leap of faith, for he knew what gravity would do to his small, frail body.

"It's time to come in, Benjamin," he would hear his mother call out to him.

With great reluctance, he would make his way inside to his bedroom, where, after being tucked in amidst the many blankets, his mother would begin the daily routine of medications. He wondered what would happen to him if he told his mother that he would no longer take them.

"C'mon, Benji, open wide," she would coax him, and like the obedient child of ten that he was, he would do so.

From his earliest memories, he knew of hospitals and emergency rooms, doctors that could only talk to his mother, nurses that smiled falsely, orderlies that would spout out jokes that meant nothing to him, all in the name of keeping him alive.

There were still the birds, fluttering around the sky, landing on the windowsill, as if to beg Ben to join them in their daily flights.

"The doctor's say that this should help with the pain," his mother would say.

Yes, there was the pain. The stinging pain that would sometimes be so intense, that he could not even bear to open his eyes. These were the hardest times, when he could not look out the window to see what his friends were up to.

"One more pill to go, son."

His mother was beautiful. Her face like an angel and her smile that could light up an entire room. Her eyes, while cheerful and bright, belied the fact that Benjamin had a very serious problem.

Even at the age of ten, he knew that he had somehow outlived what the doctors had predicted. He should have been gone a long time ago, flying with his own wings in heaven's glory.

Yes, he believed in God, and also believed that there had to be a purpose for the malady that plagued his body, requiring the numerous medications. If God had wanted him to be a healthy young boy, able to leap about and run and play, then he would have made him that way, wasn't that what the pastors and doctor's and even his mother had said?

There were sometimes when he was mad at God, but he knew that to be a sin as well, and he so wanted to go to heaven, where he could receive his wings and be able to fly like the feathered ones in the sky.

"How are you feeling today?" his mother asked.

"Ok, I guess," he replied.

"I'll have dinner ready in a little while, you just lay here and rest. You were outside pretty long today," she said as she closed his door.

It was the middle of the day, and Ben had to take a nap, to allow the medicines to work on his frail body. Oh, how he wished that he could go back outside and watch the majesty of the birds as they flew from the trees.

"Wings," he muttered, as he fell into a deep and dreamless sleep.

****

2.

"You'll be late for school."

How many times had he heard this. It had been so much easier when his mother taught him at home, learning at his own pace between medicine time and bed time. The treatments in the last three years had been of great help, yet going to a public school had turned into a nightmare.

"Did you hear me?" his mother yelled from downstairs.

"Coming!" he called out.

His mother, the beautiful angel that had taken care of him for so long, had turned old before his eyes. The toll of caring for him had ravaged her over the last three years. Wrinkles under her eyes had become more pronounced and the once trim figure had now grown in size. She wasn't fat by any means of the imagination, but she no longer sported the dancer's figure that he had remembered.

"I'm sorry," he said as he sat down for breakfast.

She placed the plate of pancakes in front of him, along with a glass of milk and a small saucer filled with the pills that prolonged his life.

"You just need to quit hitting the snooze button, honey," she said with a smile.

"Not about that, mom, about everything else," he said, taking the first pill.

She slowly sat down across from him, concern filling her eyes.

"Ben, what are you talking about?"

"Whatever happened to dad?"

A question that she had known Ben would ask someday, something that she had tried to prepare herself for.

"War, Ben, that is what happened to your father," she told him.

She went back in her mind to that dreadful day, pregnant only two months when the soldiers knocked on her door. She had seen it happen in movies and on television, had heard of the dreadful news from other Army wives who lived in the same town, but knew that it could never happen to her.

"The President regretfully announces…"

She remembered collapsing onto the porch, tears pouring down her cheeks, the feel of the soldiers hands as they tried to catch her and comfort her. She could feel the small life growing inside her and wondered what she would tell him when the time, if ever, would come when he would ask her what happened.

"I don't understand, mom," Ben said as he took another bite of pancakes, followed by another pill.

"Your father was a brave man, Ben, and he died while serving his country," she said, her voice remaining calm. She had rehearsed this so many times. She had shown Ben pictures of his father, telling him the things that he had done and how he had been so excited about her pregnancy. He had shipped out the next day and two months later, a sniper had caught him in the head.

She had never shared that part with Ben, how his father had died instantly while trying to help a small girl to cover while bullets whizzed past. The girl died when an explosion took out the building that she was running into.

She had tried not to let Benjamin know that part of the story, and gratefully, he had never asked.

Until now.

"I know that part, mom, but how exactly did he die?" he asked again, another pill disappearing into his mouth.

"Why do you need to know?" she asked.

"I was just wondering if he got his wings?"

She smiled, perhaps for the first time in three years.

"I'm sure that God gave him his wings," she told him.

"I want wings," he said without thinking.

The only thing that she could see at that moment was the small baby, fighting for its life inside an incubator at the hospital, the small frail hands reaching up, the tiny lungs grasping for each breath.

"He will be lucky to make it through the night," the doctor's had told her. By some miracle, Ben had proved all of them wrong. She knew that he was destined for great things.

"You want to be a soldier like your father?" she asked him as he ate the last bite of pancake.

"Naw, I want wings and fly," he said, almost as if he had asked her to pass the butter.

She thought that maybe he might have grown out of the obsession that he had had when he was younger, constantly watching the birds making their way to points unknown. She had even bought a bird watcher's book for him, but he had seemed uninterested in picking out the different species. He was only interested in watching them fly about the sky.

"Guess I better get going," he said as he took the empty plates to the sink. "I love you, mom," he said over his shoulder as he headed out the door.

She wondered what she could have said differently to him.

Perhaps nothing at all. Perhaps nothing more needed to be said, but the thing about the birds and flying had actually started to worry her.

Getting up from the table, she made her way to the living room, pouring a glass of bourbon into a tall glass and trying to drink the memory of her husband, the war hero, who had died in a senseless way, out of her mind.

She had tried to be sober, or at least sober enough, when Benji got home from school. Most days, she could fake her way through and take care of the household and the bills. Lately, as Ben got older, the drinking had become more and more prevalent. No longer was she hiding the bottles around the house.

"War," she muttered as she took another long drink.

Softly, she began to cry.

****

3.

“You going to the party tonight?”

Ben’s best friend Larry had often talked about the parties that he claimed to be at. At seventeen, only a year older than Ben, the way he talked, he had been partying since he was three years old.

“Lots of college girls there tonight, so you should really come,” Larry told him, his back against the wall as he was sprawled on Ben’s bed.

“I don’t think mom would let me,” Ben said, “besides, I have therapy tonight.”

“He probably won’t make it to sixteen,” the doctor’s had said. The pills had begun to have a detrimental effect on his immune system and he had spent two months in the hospital. The next step was the therapy that had become a weekly thing. The only part of it was the pretty nurse that helped him. She reminded him of how his mom had used to be and how she had been so beautiful.

“What party?” Ben’s mom said from the doorway.

Ben looked up from the homework that he was working on and saw the hair, unkempt and mussed, the flabbiness of the arms and the smell of alcohol that seemed to permeate from every pore.

“Nothing mom, someplace that Larry’s going to,” he told her.

“You got therapy tonight, remember?” she said, her words slurring a little.

“It’s okay, I’ll get there. I’ve already called a cab,” he told her.

“Because you know that I can’t drive you,” she continued, “and I don’t think that I would even if I could.”

Larry felt the vibe in the room change and could tell the hurt look on Ben’s face. He was sure that he had never heard Ben’s mom say anything hurtful to him, at least not while he was there, and

Ben had never mentioned that there was any trouble at home.

"Listen, Ben, I gotta go if I'm going to make that party. Catch you later," Larry said as he got off the bed. "Bye."

"Mom, what are saying?"

"I don't know," she said as she heard the door close from downstairs. "Maybe it would have been better if you had died. Maybe I could have found a man to take care of me, don't you understand? The doctor's didn't give you a chance in the hospital, but here you are, sixteen years later, still hanging on. What the hell are you waiting for! Why don't you go ahead and get your damn wings!"

Ben had never heard any of this before and it hurt him in the worst way. Slamming his pencil onto the desk, he stood up, his body still frail and weak, but his eyes were burning with tears and rage.

"Stop it! I know that I should be dead, and maybe tomorrow you won't have to worry anymore!" he screamed, grabbing his coat and running out into the night.

How easy it would be to go to the old wooden bridge, stretch out his hands and jump into nothingness. How many times had he thought about doing just that in the last three years? All the pain would be gone, his mother no longer burdened with the pain of watching him hover between life and death. No more pills or treatments or doctor's or anything that would keep him from getting his wings.

He saw the bird through the tears in his eyes. It was small and frail, like him, but its wings were strong and flew up into the night sky, disappearing among the shadows.

His mind traveled back to the summer days when he was allowed to lay out on the lawn and be content at watching the birds. The thoughts of flight flooded him again as he found himself at the old wooden bridge, looking down into the rushing waters.

"I want my wings!"

****

4.

The tassle on the cap that sat on Ben's head was blowing into his face. The gown that he wore was flimsy, but he was proud of the moment that had come at last.

College had been hard, between the classes and the studying, along with the treatments that he was now taking every other day, but somehow he had made it to this day.

Scanning the audience, he finally was able to see his mom. She looked radiant, like she had when he was ten. Five years of sobriety had helped her looks, even though her hair had started to turn grey. She had been able to stay on the diet and away from the bottle, even though there had been days when she would have gladly jumped headfirst off of the wagon.

He had been so proud of her and now she was even more proud of him.

As they announced his name, he slowly rose up to receive the document that he had worked so hard for.

The itching on his shoulders had begun again. As he walked along the platform, he could hardly contain the discomfort and he wiggled his shoulders, trying to make the itching go away, but there wasn't anything that he could do.

Accepting the document and a handshake from the professor's, he made his way back to his seat. A few minutes later, the caps flew into the air.

"So, party tonight?" Larry asked him.

They had both enrolled and had gotten accepted into the same college and had remained friends the entire time.

"Naw, I need to be with mom tonight, you know how it is," Ben told him.

"What are your plans tonight, son?" his mother asked as she

approached the pair. "Seeing some nice young girl?" she asked with a slight grin.

"You look good," Larry commented, making her blush.

"Hey, dude," Ben said sternly, "that's my mom."

"And a very hot mom it is," Larry said with another grin.

"I thought I might stay with you tonight, mom," Ben said.

She looked at Ben and said, "Honey, I'm fine. You go and have a good time. I'll be fine, even if you don't come home until the morning."

"Are you sure?"

"Even a mother bird teaches her young to fly," she said with a smile.

He loved his mother so much, and could feel the tears welling up for the hard work that she had done not only for him, but for herself.

"Okay, but only if your sure," Ben said.

"Go," she told him.

It would be the last thing that he heard from her.

It was three in the morning when Larry finally dropped him off at his home. The house was silent. No lights had been on anywhere. Calling out when he opened the door, he immediately knew that something was very wrong.

He had found her lying on the sofa, a bottle of whiskey in one hand, a bottle of pills in the other. The note that lay on the floor beside her had only said that she loved him, but it was time for him to fly.

The myriad amount of people that had come into the house that early morning were soon to be a fading memory. Questions that he could not answer had been asked without results. There had been talk of charging him with something like manslaughter but were quickly dismissed.

At the age of 25, Ben only wanted to fly, like his mother wanted.

The strange sensation in his shoulders had grown more pronounced, as if something were growing, trying to force its way outside of his body.

Wings?

As he sat on the very sofa that once held the body of his mother, still warm from her mortal form, the thought of him actually growing wings and being able to fly overwhelmed him. He wondered, now that the men from the county had taken her away, would she finally be with his dad, her wings touching his as they made their way through heaven? The thought comforted him in one way, and yet, in another way, he wished that he did have wings, for now, he wanted to fly, away from this place of death that had once held happy memories.

The funeral was peaceful. There had only been a few people there, mostly from the AA meetings that his mother had attended. Larry had been there, although he had to fly to Boston for a job that he had gotten directly out of college. Ben had been very grateful that he had been there.

"Why don't you come to Boston with me?" Larry had asked after the burial.

"I have too much to do here," Ben had told him.

"Well, the invite still stands. If you need anything, don't hesitate to call me, okay?"

Trying to pack up the house had been more of a chore than even Ben had expected. Without any other family members, he managed to get rid of the things that had piled up around the home. There were still a few things that he kept, mostly small things that would not take up much room.

The house had been paid for a long time ago, and was his if he wanted to stay.

As he sat on the sofa, he looked at the vastness of the home. So many memories, so many things said both in anger and in happier times. He had wished that he could live it all over again, watching his mother come down the stairs, calling him in for dinner, making sure that his medication was correct. It was all becoming too much for him to take.

He found himself walking toward the old wooden bridge, stopping at the edge and looking down into the churning water of the river below. For the second time, he had contemplated taking the leap and at least feeling the sensation of flying.

The bumps on his shoulders were larger now, and he wondered if he should mention them to the doctor's that he saw now.

****

5.

"Why can't you get a better job?"

Ben was 37, married, with a dead end job, not enough money, never anything that would satisfy his wife, and he was tired.

"Don't forget the party tonight," she would say.

"I have my treatment tonight," he would tell her.

"Your treatment? What about me? Don't you ever think about me?"

It had turned into the same argument practically every night.

"Besides, maybe your boss will notice that you are more important to the company than they realize and you could get somewhere."

This was simply her way of saying that he wasn't important to anyone and that he would never be able to afford the things that she really wanted.

"Have you ever noticed the birds?" he asked.

"What are you talking about?"

"The way they fly and flit about in the trees. Their song that seems to welcome in the spring…"

"Don't be poetic dear, it does not become you. Why I ever married you I can't understand."

That was it. After seven years of hearing her, he had had enough.

"You married me, my sweet, because I was stupid enough to ask you. You accepted because you thought that you could not do any better than a loser like me. Now, if you don't mind, I'm going out."

He had left her with her mouth agape and speechless.

"Why can't I just fly away?" he asked himself.

He had kept the house and seven years ago, after the marriage, he had moved this woman into the home that he had grown up in. She had immediately changed everything, taking out all of the furniture that had been left and running up bills as if he were the president of the company instead of a mail room clerk.

The itching in his shoulders had started again.

For a while, the sensation had gone away. After the marriage, he had thought that it had gone permanently, but in the last few weeks, since the fighting had begun, the slight pain of something just below the skin had come back.

He was back at the old wooden bridge. Looking into the water, he spied a family of birds nesting just below the bridge. He ached to be with them, wanting to feel the cool spray of the river glide across his wings.

Yes, wings, that was what he wanted. Large, beautiful white gossamer wings that would allow him to leave the earth and fly into the sky, skimming the waters of rivers, lakes, and oceans, letting him feel the wind on his face as he floated lazily across the clouds. It was what he had always dreamed of, ever since he laid on the lawn and watched the birds fly on their endless journey's to nowhere.

"Where the hell have you been?" his wife had said as he entered their home.

"Out."

"Brilliant, that tells me everything. What are you doing?"

What he was doing was raising his shoulders up by his ears, slowly letting them down.

"I figure that I have to develop some strong muscle to be able to flap them, if they ever come."

She only looked stupidly at him, a look that he had once admired.

"What are you talking about?"

"My wings. I can feel them coming and I need to start developing my shoulders if I'm ever going to be able to fly."

"It's finally happened. You have gone insane. Too much licking stamps in that hell hole that you call work?"

"I don't expect you to understand. I think that my mom did,

she just didn't want to tell me. She knew that sometimes the mother bird has to let go and let the young one discover certain things for itself."

"You really are off your rocker. Do you mean to tell me that you are actually thinking that you can grow a set of wings?"

"I told you that you would not understand," Ben said, continuing to raise his shoulders up and down.

****

6.

"Ben, get down from there!"

His wife was standing on the driveway, looking up at him.

It had been two weeks since he first decided to grow his wings. Every day, instead of going to the clinic for his daily treatments, he was jogging, trying to develop his lungs so that he could take the thinner air that he knew must be up there. Many people would watch him as he would flap his arms, trying to strengthen his muscles. After a week of doing this, Ben noticed that other jogger's had started to do the same thing. Perhaps they also had decided to grow wings. He imagined an entire flock of joggers suddenly taking off from the park and circling the sky above the city, and it made him smile.

"I said, get down from up there!" she screamed at him.

"I need to get the feel before the wings start coming in. I figure if I land from up here, it won't hurt as much."

"What's going on?" one of the neighbors asked.

"Nothing, nothing," he heard his wife say.

"Hey, Frank, I'm trying out a landing before my wings come in," Ben yelled down.

Ben's wife was mortified at what he had just said and tried to laugh it off.

"He means, um, um, sky diving!" she blurted out.

"Great sport," Frank said, "if you have the courage."

"Yes," she continued, "and you have to practice landing before they will allow you to jump, you know?"

"Yes, I have heard of that. But I thought he said something about wings?" Frank asked.

"Yes, well, um, he meant a parachute," she tried to cover.

Ben began to flap his arms up and down.

"What's he doing now?" Frank asked.

By now, several of the neighbors had gathered in the street and were looking at the strange frail man that was standing on the roof, flapping his arms like a giant bird. A look of expectation covered his features as if he was waiting for the wind to take him from the earthly bounds of gravity.

Ben's wife covered her mouth, her eyes wide with astonishment.

"What is Ben doing?" a neighbor from across the street asked Frank.

"His wife says that he is practicing for a parachute jump," Frank answered.

"No, I mean, what is he doing with his arms?" the neighbor asked.

"Beats me. Hey, what is your husband doing with his arms?" Frank asked Ben's wife.

She turned from the scene that her own husband was causing and looked upon the scene of the entire neighborhood staring and pointing up at the roof. She wasn't sure which one was the most embarrassing and would have given anything to find a nearby hole in which to crawl into.

"I think," she started slowly, "that it is an exercise that he was told to do."

"Yea," one of the others mentioned, "I saw him doing that very thing the other day while he was jogging. I've seen others doing it as well. I think it helps with the circulation."

Thank God for small favors. Ben had been seen by someone else and it seemed that other people had been flapping their arms. Perhaps the situation wasn't as bad as she thought.

Until Ben decided to open his mouth and yell out, "I'm going to sprout wings!"

The laughter was sparse, at first, and then became an uproar.

"Oh, Ben," his wife said as the tears began to flow. She shook her head and made her way inside.

****

7.

"I hope that you are satisfied," she said as Ben finally came inside.

The sky was darkening and the streetlights were beginning to flicker to life. The neighbors had made their way back into their homes and their lives. Tomorrow, at least Ben's wife had hoped, they would forget all about the incident that had transpired.

Ben wasn't listening. He was too busy. He made his way throughout the house, hurriedly and with purpose, gathering things here and there and depositing them onto the kitchen table where his wife was sitting, gulping down a very large whiskey.

"Ben, what are you doing now? Have you taken your medications today?"

"I need some things. I believe that it might be cold tonight," Ben said as he threw another armful of things onto the table. Again, he made his way throughout the house.

Standing up, Ben's wife stood and blocked his pathway to the table that was already piled high with varying things that, when put together, made no sense at all.

"Excuse me for prying," she began, a slight edge to her voice, "but exactly what are your intentions with all of these things?"

"Nesting," he said, breezing past her and putting more things down onto the table.

"I'm sorry, I don't think I quite heard you," she said as he sailed past her and into the den.

"Well," he told her, "I'm going to need some blankets and maybe some food and some sort of entertainment. I'm thinking of the elm that stands in the front yard. I saw a lot of birds building their nests there over the years, so it must be a pretty good place. Besides, my wings should come in any day and I want to be ready."

"Would it help everything along if I saved you the trouble and just went completely crazy now?" his wife asked. "What the hell are you talking about?" she screamed.

Without another word, Ben had gathered the various things and made his way to the front yard.

"Wait, Ben!" she called out.

By the time that she had made her way outside, Ben was already halfway up the giant elm tree. He was looking for the perfect branch and he was sure that he could find it. He had seen a family of robin's nesting there only two months ago. How he had wished to be with them.

"Ben!"

She heard a door open and close and realized that Frank was on his way back to find out what lunacy was happening this time. She couldn't take another bout of this and quickly made her way back inside.

Opening the curtains, she watched in abject horror as her husband began laying things across the large branches of the tree that was most certainly situated in their front yard, and the slowly gathering throng of neighbors that once again were gathering to see this strange sight. She didn't know what story she might tell them. The man that she had shared a home and a life with had obviously gone off of his rocker and...

Yes, that was it, she thought.

She closed the curtain, picked up the phone, and dialed 911.

****

8.

Ben was quite comfortable. He had never built a nest before and thought that he had done a pretty decent job of it. There was no way that he was going to fall to the ground, not the way that he had tied the blankets around the varying branches of the large elm. He was extremely proud of the work that he had finally finished.

"This is the police, sir. Are you injured in any way?"

Ben lifted his head and peered down into the throng of people that had gathered at the base of the tree. He looked out into the street and saw the three police cars and single ambulance that had parked in front of his house, their lights flashing on and off, causing weird shadows against the grass and the side of the house.

He saw his wife, a look of triumph on her face, standing in the doorway.

"I'm perfectly fine," Ben yelled down. He had not realized that he was probably forty feet off the ground, high up in the confines of the tree.

"Is there anything you would like to talk about?" the policeman yelled up at him.

"Nothing that comes to mind right now, however, if you want to hang around for a little while, I might think of something. Perhaps you might come up with something to discuss later on, but right now, I'm a little busy," Ben told them and began to busy himself by placing things in small, tight area's that he had created with the blankets.

"Yea, he's a raving loony, all right," the officer that had talked said to his partner. "Better get the ambulance on standby and call the psychiatric ward."

"How are you going to get him down?" Frank, the neighbor

asked.

A puzzled look crossed the face of the officer.

"Well, we'll just…" the officer started, but realized that he did not have a good answer. It wasn't like he could pull out his service revolver and shoot the man down.

The officer hated calls like this. Give him a guy coming at him with a knife or a gun any day and he was quite happy. But no, he always got the loonies, he lamented to himself.

"Sir," the officer yelled up at Ben again, "why don't you come down and we can have a nice chat?"

Ben looked down at the officer again and said, "I told you, I'm a little busy right now. Besides, am I breaking any laws?"

The officer couldn't think of one law that Ben was breaking. So what if a guy wants to camp out in the upper branches of a tree that sits on his own property, who should care? There had been many nights when, after a fierce battle with his own wife, he had wished that he had built a treehouse to run away to.

"You may hurt yourself, sir!" the officer tried.

Ben thought a moment and said, "Only if I'm unfortunate to fall and someone is unfortunately standing under me, in which case, I would yell for them to move before I actually hit them."

Sounded reasonable to the officer.

"Besides," Ben continued, "I expect my wings would break any fall in which I might be involved in."

"Sure, your," the officer started and then paused. "What did you say?"

Was everyone deaf, Ben thought before he yelled down, "My wings!"

The officer turned toward the woman standing in the doorway of the house and smiled.

"Better get the strait jacket for this one," the officer told the medics that were now convinced they would have a customer any moment now.

"Sir, I think that it would be best for everyone if you were to come down and explain exactly what you mean by your wings," the officer tried.

"I would really like to help you officer, but as you can see, I have constructed my nest and am ready to get a little shut eye. I'm not sure when my wings will appear, but I am sure that it is going to be soon and I want to be ready," Ben yelled down just before settling into the warmth of the nest.

At this point, the blare of a fire truck, complete with ladder, pulled into the melee of on-lookers. Firemen, ready for action, began to pull things from the truck. The captain had pulled in behind the truck and was busy putting on his coat, looking for whoever happened to be in charge so that he could take over the situation.

"Officer, want to give me an update on the hostage," the captain said.

"What hostage?" the officer asked.

"I was told that a man was holding his wife hostage up in a tree somewhere," the captain said.

"No," the officer began, "the wife called us and said that her husband was up a tree."

"So the man is crazy. What is he armed with?" the captain said.

"Nothing, he is literally up a tree," the officer said, pointing to said tree.

The captain smirked.

"You've been drinking?" he asked the officer.

"Just look!"

The captain looked at where the man was pointing. His grin turned to astonishment as he saw the intricate pattern of blankets that crossed several branches. He could not see any man.

"So we have been sent here at great city expense to rescue some wayward laundry?" the captain said.

The officer wanted to smash the man's nose in, but instead, yelled up at the tree, "Hey, sir, would you mind explaining to the fire department what they are doing here?"

Ben was puzzled. He looked down at the ever growing throng of people and said, "Why, is something on fire? Did my wife try to cook again?"

He remembered the last time she had tried to create a gourmet meal and wound up burning down half the kitchen.

The captain looked at the officer, who simply looked back at him.

"What the hell is he doing up there?" the captain asked.

"Waiting to sprout wings," the officer said before walking back to his car for a stiff drink from the flask that he carried in the glove compartment.

Ben simply laid back and closed his eyes. His shoulders had begun to ache from all of the flapping that he had been doing earlier. He wondered if birds ever got tired and aching muscles. Perhaps that was why they nested so much.

Opening his eyes again, he could see the rising moon through the branches and the many stars that dotted the heaven above him. He could not wait to get his wings and fly towards the moon, watching the landscape below him pass by in a rush.

He closed his eyes again and went to sleep.

****

9.

Flying.

Feeling the wind sweeping across his face, looking down at the ground as it passes by, the sensation was almost overwhelming. He watched the clouds pass overhead and soared as high as his wings would take him. He dove into a valley and skimmed the floor, barely touching the ground. Just before crashing into the wall of the canyon, he shot straight up into the air, emerging like a giant eagle, soaring higher and higher.

Ben smiled.

His wings were magnificent, much grander than he could ever imagine. His body felt weightless as he glided throughout the streets, seeing the people below pointing up at him.

No, wait, something was going wrong.

He felt himself falling, as if his wings were no longer there where they had always been. He began flapping his arms madly, trying to force himself away from the approaching ground.

No, he wasn't flying, and had never been.

He was…he was…

****

10.

"It took some doing, but we waited for the subject to fall asleep before attempting to bring him out of the tree. I would like to thank the fire department for their valiant effort in bringing the subject down."

The officer was very proud of himself. He thought about the promotion that he might get after his superiors saw the interview on the late night news.

"Exactly what was the subject doing in the tree in the first place? ", the pretty young girl from the news team asked. "Were any weapons found on him?"

"No, no weapons were found. He was just up a tree," the officer said into the camera.

"So what crime was committed?" the girl asked.

Ah, yes, well there was that, wasn't there. As far as the officer was concerned, no crime had actually been committed. What was he going to say now? He could see his promotion drifting away from him.

"Well, no crime per se, however, his wife did feel that he might be in danger and it is our sworn duty to not only uphold the law, but to protect the citizens of this great city," the officer said.

Yes, he felt pretty good about that.

"Does the police have a policy of making sure that people do not climb trees on their own property?" the girl asked.

"Well..."

"This is Eyewitness News. Okay, cut, that's a wrap. Thanks officer," the girl said as she rolled up the microphone cord and headed back toward the news van.

The officer really hated the news. At least the subject was safely out of the tree, into an ambulance heading toward the hospital and was now someone else's problem.

****

11.

"Why do you think that you are a bird?"

The man in the horn rimmed glasses sat across from Ben at his desk, slowly drawing something on a pad of paper. He seemed very disinterested in the whole business.

"That sounds crazy," Ben said. "I don't think that I'm a bird."

"Then why were you in the tree?" horn rimmed glasses said.

"I told everyone, including my shrew of a wife, why I was in the tree," Ben answered.

"Ah, yes, you said that you were waiting for your wings. Exactly what did you mean by that?" horn rimmed glasses said.

"What do you think I mean?" Ben asked.

Horned rimmed looked up from his doodle of a huge bird with a man's face, startled that the subject had asked him something.

"Pardon me?" horned rimmed asked.

"I said," Ben began, "why do you think I would say such a thing to a crowd of people while being in a tree?"

"I don't think I can answer that unless you answer my question."

"So, what was your question?"

Horned rimmed now looked concerned. This was not going the exact way that he thought it should. He tried a different approach.

"How did you feel while you were in the tree?" horned rimmed asked.

"How do you feel sitting behind a desk?" Ben countered.

No, not going well at all.

"You are being antagonistic. Now why don't you answer my questions?"

"Why don't you answer mine?"

"Do you wish to go home?" horned rimmed asked.

Ben thought for a moment. Oh yes, home, home up in the sky, flying with his friends, the only friends that he seemed to have his entire life. He desperately wanted to be with them, to glide along the oceans and the mountains and to see life from a distance.

"Do you think that you are a bird?" horned rimmed asked.

"That would be crazy if I did, wouldn't it?" Ben asked.

"Why don't you tell me," horned rimmed said.

"No, I'm not a bird. I don't really know why I'm here. I was simply laying in a tree on my own property. I did not realize that it was a crime. What do you think?" Ben asked.

"I think," horned rimmed said, "that we should keep you here for at least 72 hours."

****

12.

Three days seemed to go by quickly, at the end of which, Ben was met by his wife at the entrance to the hospital.

"I want you to know, that I cannot and will not do this anymore. My attorney says that I could get everything if we can prove you incompetent. So no more of this business of wings and flying and such nonsense. When we get home, you are going to start your therapy again and behave in a normal manner or so help me I'll…"

Ben turned on her.

"You will do what? Have me thrown back into a psychiatric ward? I wish that you of all people could understand. I don't belong here. I've known that all of my life."

His wife turned red in the face.

"Ben, the divorce papers will be in the mail. Until then, you can stay at a motel," she said, leaving him on the curb as she drove away.

He ran.

He ran and ran, flapping his arms madly, willing his wings to appear.

Nothing.

No, he thought, it wasn't fair. He did not belong on the ground, he knew this. He needed to be in the sky, flying free.

His lungs began to hurt, his breath coming in shorter bursts. Behind him, he heard the horn blasting just before the car hit him.

****

13.

He felt the pain in his bones, especially the two broken ones. He slowly opened his eyes and saw the police officer standing over him.

"Your wife is in custody. All we need is your signature on the complaint and we can put her away for a long time."

"No," Ben managed to say.

"But she tried to kill you, sir."

"She just didn't understand. It will be all right, she will, and very soon."

The officer shrugged his shoulders and left the room.

"Somehow, I'll make her understand," Ben said thoughtfully.

****

14.

"Thank you for not having me arrested, Ben," his wife said after he returned home from the hospital three weeks later.

"I just need you to understand."

"I'll try," she told him, sipping a cup of coffee. She had stopped drinking and had patiently waited for her husband to return home. All thoughts of divorce had left her mind when she had heard the sickening thud of his body against the grill of the car. It had not been her intention to run him down, only to catch up with him. He was swerving left just as she had swerved right.

The flapping of his arms had been a bit of a distraction.

"Ever since I was young, I have been sick. I have been through medicines, treatments, doctors who knew everything and nothing, and the only thing that ever made me happy, was watching the birds. I felt that I was a part of their tribe, that somehow, when I was born, I was supposed to be a bird.

"I know now that it wasn't just a bird that I was to become, but that I was to have wings in which to fly and be a part of their world. I felt the wings trying to come through so that I could take flight and leave the earth, but every time I try to force them out, nothing happens."

His wife sat quietly until he was finished. After a few moments, she set her coffee down on the table and looked at her husband with deep purpose in her eyes.

"Ben, I want you to listen very carefully. While you were in the hospital, the doctors did a lot of x-rays on most of your body, including your shoulders and back. They found a strange growth of bone just above the spine and spreading out toward your shoulders."

Ben began to move his shoulder blades up and down. Something was very strange and very, very wrong.

His wife continued.

"They sent the x-rays to a bone specialist and he sent back a report. Ben, it was some sort of cancerous growth that probably started when you were very young. No one caught it because they did not know it was there. The operation was successful and they even said that it might have been what was causing you to be so sick all of these years."

Ben tried reaching behind him, feeling up toward where his wings should have been. Instead, he felt the bandage and the stitches that he knew were underneath it.

"So you see," his wife continued, "everything is going to be fine. The growth has been sent to the specialist and he should contact us with the results in just a few days."

"What have you done?" he asked, his voice quivering slightly.

"Honey, I did what I thought was best," she said soothingly.

Ben jumped up from the chair, his bandaged legs screaming in pain.

"What have you done!" he yelled at her.

****

15.

The birds were beginning to fly south for the winter. The days were getting shorter and the nights longer and Ben could only sit at the window and watch them as they flew past, leaving him behind.

There had been no word from the specialist for three weeks and Ben's wife was beginning to worry. All calls to his office were met with the phrase that the doctor was busy and would contact them as soon as he could.

"Ben? Do you want something to eat?" she asked.

Ben sat silently.

"Honey?"

He would not answer her. He had not spoken to her since that night when he learned that his wings had been clipped, that he was now earthbound forever.

She could not believe that he was still upset with her. Had she not saved his life? Perhaps the growths were some sort of cancer and somehow they had been removed in the nick of time.

Ben watched the sky and saw the birds flying so high and free. How he wanted to be there with them, flying and swooping and soaring.

He first felt the protrusion as a red cardinal landed on the branch of the tree that stood outside his window. The small ache in his back became more pronounced as a robin landed beside the cardinal. They seemed to be beckoning to him, to join them in their quest for a warmer climate.

He heard the slight tearing sound of his skin as a swallow, grayish in color landed between the cardinal and robin. Its small beady eyes looked directly at Ben, as if a thought were passing between them.

Ben slowly stood up, the bandages falling away from his legs. He felt a new found strength as the first feather tickled his neck. The tearing of his skin caused him no pain, just a dull throb as the tip of the first wing made its way out of his body.

A wren landed next to the others and seemed to give Ben the courage to make his way towards the door. The four birds watched as the wings became more pronounced.

A finch now joined the others and flapped madly about on the branch. Ben smiled at his new found friends. He could see the reflection of himself in the hallway mirror that his wife had insisted on putting up. Just above his shoulders, he could see the tips of something white and feathery. He could feel the softness of the protrusions on the opening of his skin.

Perhaps the only thing that was preventing him from getting his wings was the growth that the doctors had removed. Whatever the circumstances, he knew that his wings were coming into shape, greeting the world.

A bob white landed next to the others and produced his customary greeting to Ben. He seemed to be pleased with this new creature that was soon to join them in the night sky.

Ben made his way toward the front door, stepping out into the cool air. He could feel the wings growing from out of his back, the ache giving way to a more pleasant sensation of freedom.

No neighbors this time to look at him and point and laugh. This time, he knew where to go.

He made his way towards the old wooden bridge.

The birds took flight and followed.

****

16.

"I don't think that you are going to believe me," the specialist said.

Ben's wife had heard the phone ring just as she was bringing her husband something to eat, even though he had not said anything. For three weeks she had done what she could for him, but nothing seemed to be right.

"Just tell me, doctor, what did you find?" she asked him anxiously.

"Well, the bone is exactly that, just bone. Nothing cancerous about it, thank God."

"But you don't sound too convinced," she told him.

"Well, it's the type of bone that you had the hospital send me. Are you sure that this came from your husband?" he asked her.

"I suppose, the hospital took care of all of that. Why do you ask?"

"Then someone at the hospital is playing a pretty sick joke on me," the specialist said.

"What do you mean?"

"Whoever packaged the sample sent me the bone from the wing of a bird."

****

17.

Ben's wife found herself running. She could hear the distant call of the specialist from the phones receiver that she had dropped to the kitchen floor.

She ran first into the room where Ben had been staring out of the window. He was gone, and for one dreadful moment, she thought of him up on the roof again, his arms flapping madly, only this time, he would jump and land hard onto the ground.

She ran outside and looked around the rooftop, yelling his name over and over again.

Frank drove up and rolled his window down.

"What's going on?" Frank asked.

"Have you seen Ben?"

"As a matter of fact, I saw him heading toward the old wooden bridge. Why do you ask?"

Without answering, she began to run, faster and faster, hoping to catch Ben before he did anything stupid, like jumping from the bridge thinking that he could actually fly.

"Ben!"

She saw him at the end of the bridge, looking down into the water far below. She watched in fascination as he looked up into the sky. She saw him turn and face her, a glowing smile on his face.

"I got them!"

****

18.

"And you say he actually took flight?" the man with the horned rimmed glasses asked her.

"Yes, he did. He just lifted up off the ground, a huge pair of white wings folding outward, like an angel. I saw his body grow smaller and smaller. I saw the beak start where his mouth was. I saw my husband turn into an eagle."

The man with the horned rimmed glasses quietly closed the door to the patients room, a permanent resident of the psychiatric ward.

He walked back to his office where a police detective waited.

"Well, what do you think, doc?" the detective asked.

"I believe that she is suffering a mental breakdown from the act of killing her husband. As you recall, she tried to run him down not too long ago and when that did not work, she pushed him off the bridge. Did you find the body?" the horned rimmed glasses asked.

"No, but that is not too unusual. He'll probably wash up somewhere down river. We did find one curious thing."

"Yes, what was that?" the doctor asked.

The detective pulled out a long plastic evidence bag. Inside was a long white feather.

"Someone on scene identified it as an eagle feather. Funny thing, there hasn't been an eagle seen in this area for over fifty years."

The doctor only nodded.

****

19.

The eagle sat on the power line directly across from the doctors window. He cocked his head to one side as if to hear what the two men were saying. He saw the detective shake his head slowly as he placed the evidence bag back into his pocket.

He stretched his wings outward, hesitating as his eyes caught the lone figure of a woman that he once called his wife, staring at him.

"Ben?" she whispered softly.

With one shrill cry, the eagle took flight into the night sky.

****

Prolouge

The butler did it.

####

This was a quick story and one in which I hope that you enjoyed reading. It did not involve serial killers, sex, violence, or crime of any kind. It was basically an experiment to see what I could come up with. I hope that you enjoyed it, dear reader, and that you will give some of my other works a chance to catch you in their grip. I would like to dedicate this story to four people. One is the finest cook that I have ever had the pleasure of delighting in her cuisine, the second is my best friend, the third is my collaborator, and the fourth is my companion and who, without her insight, I would never had come up with the ending to this story. All of them is actually one person. I love you, Starshine.

Until next time...
Winslow Swan

Please check out my other works of fiction
The Convincer
Click (A Tale Of Revenge)
Toppling Over The Edge
Thank you again for all of your support and please pass this story onto others.